I am a reader and I celebrated
World Book Day 2023 with this
gift from my local bookseller
and Faber.

....

WORLD BOOK DAY®

World Book Day's mission is to offer every child and young person the opportunity to read and love books by giving you the chance to have a book of your own.

To find out more, and for fun activities including the monthly World Book Day Book Club, video stories and book recommendations, visit **worldbookday.com**

World Book Day is a charity sponsored by National Book Tokens.

DAVE Pigeon
Bookshop Mayhem!

Dave Pigeon's Book on
How to Write a
World Book Day Book

Typed up by Skipper

(with a little bit of help from
Swapna Haddow and
Sheena Dempsey)

faber

This book is dedicated to you.
Yes! YOU! Happy World Book Day
from every single pigeon in the world
including Gaz from down the road.
SH & SD

First published in 2023 by
Faber and Faber Limited, Bloomsbury House
74–77 Great Russell Street, London WC1B 3DA

Designed by Faber
Printed and bound in the UK by
CPI Group (UK) Ltd, Croydon, CR0 4YY

A CIP record for this book is available from the British Library

ISBN 978-0-571-38032-9

MIX
Paper | Supporting
responsible forestry
FSC® C171272

Printed and bound in the UK on FSC paper in line with our continuing
commitment to ethical business practices, sustainability and the environment.
For further information see faber.co.uk/environmental-policy

2 4 6 8 10 9 7 5 3 1

1
Who Put a Couple of Pigeons in Charge of Writing a World Book Day Book?

'How about a pigeontastic adventure involving a grey slipper?'

'A slipper?' I asked.

'Slippers can be very interesting once you get to know them,' Dave replied.

'So what happens with this slipper?' I said, as I tapped on the keys of our typewriter.

'I can't come up with everything myself!' Dave huffed throwing his head back in frustration.

I looked at the balled-up scraps of paper littering our shed floor. Writing a brand-new story was impossible.

We'd given up on the story about the time we saw a cloud that looked a bit like Dave's granny's bottom. We'd ditched the story about the time we thought we were being chased by a lion that turned out to be a tree. And now there was Dave's slipper story ...

I ripped out Dave's ridiculous suggestion from the typewriter roller and tossed it over my shoulder to join the rest of the rubbish ideas on the ground.

'It's World Book Day tomorrow!' I cried. 'We need a story.'

'Don't you think I know that, Skipper?' Dave groaned. 'My pigeon fans will be wanting to know what I've been up to for the last couple of years.'

His shoulders slumped as he plodded down from the window ledge to join me on the shed bench. 'They'll want to hear stories of how I vanquished megalodons—'

'No one would ever think you did that, Dave.'

'And they'll want to read about how I dived head first into an erupting volcano—'

'Dave, you couldn't dive head first into that pot of paint over there,' I said, pointing at the can on the floor.

'That's because the lid has been painted shut,' Dave scoffed. 'Otherwise I could.' He couldn't. He tried earlier this morning.

Despite Dave's bonkers ideas, he *did* have a point. We'd told everyone we'd gone on holiday. We'd hoped to return with wingfuls of adventures and

tales to tell. But the truth is we got about as far as the bakery at the end of the street and then just spent our entire holiday eating croissant scraps.

Best holiday of my life.

Sadly, the bakery closed down and with it our lifetime supply of burnt pastry bits. We'd returned home to our Human Lady's shed only to find she had gone off on holiday too.

I plumped up an old cushion for Dave to nest in. As he faffed and fussed, I searched our shed. Surely, there was a story right here.

I paced the long edge of the bench and looked at the wonky shelves full of boring odds and ends. There were jars of boring nails, old boring plant pots, boring rusty tools and a boring pile of boring cables that led to boring nowhere.

I flew up to the window ledge and looked out into the garden. The grass hadn't been mown since the Human Lady had gone away last week but it was still short. There were a couple of boring ladybirds teetering on the edge of a boring blade of grass by the boring bird bath.

'I wish there was a place full of books and we could just pretend we wrote one of them,' Dave moaned, interrupting my thoughts. His tummy grumbled in unison. 'And somewhere we could get a biscuit or two as well.'

I stopped pacing.

'Dave,' I grinned. 'You are a genius.'

2
Skipper Has a Great Idea for the World Book Day Story

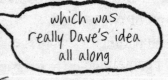

which was
really Dave's idea
all along

'Are we going with the slipper story?' Dave asked hopefully.

'No,' I said, swooping over to help him up from his cushion nest. 'I have a better idea. We're going to *find* our story.'

'Are we going to find biscuits too?' he asked, though I could barely hear him over the angry gurgle rumbling from his tummy.

'Biscuits too,' I confirmed.

'Where are we going?' Dave said, following me across the shed towards the open panel in the wooden door.

'We are going to the one place there are books *and* biscuits.'

'The toilet?'

I looked him straight in the eyes. 'Why would there be books and biscuits in a toilet?'

'In case you were in there a while,' he said with authority.

'We are not going to a toilet,' I sighed.

'The bus stop?' he asked.

'Why would there be books and biscuits at a bus stop?' I exclaimed.

'Because there might be a toilet there,' Dave replied.

'We are going to a *bookshop*,' I interrupted, before Dave could suggest another catbrained idea.

Catbrained?! I never had a catbrained idea in my life!

How about the time you suggested that if we run backwards fast enough we might be able to turn back time and we could eat those day-old croissants all over again?

It was a good idea.

It didn't work.

You weren't running fast enough, Skipper.

'Let's go to the bookshop by the zoo,' Dave said, excitedly. 'I've seen the biscuits they stash there.'

'My thoughts exactly,' I said.

Dave and I knew this bookshop well. We'd popped over one time and seen an entire crate of the biscuits with the jam in the middle – my favourites. But we'd been chased out by the Human Bookseller With A Beard before we managed to get our wings on the crumbly treats.

This time, though, we were not going to leave empty-winged.

The bookshop wasn't far from our shed. We hitched a ride part of the way in the basket under a Little Human's pushchair – before we were shooed away by a Human Mum who was looking for the rice cakes we had just eaten.

We travelled the last part of the High Street on the bus, following the signs for the zoo, and hopped off when we saw the swirly 'Z O O' letters on large, wrought-iron gates.

'Biscuits!' Dave drooled, his wings trembling with excitement.

We crossed over the road and headed straight for the open doors of the bookshop.

Dave skipped up to the door, whistling all the way across the large green doormat. Then he halted so suddenly I almost barrelled into him.

There, blocking his route in, was a boot belonging to the Human Bookseller With A Beard.

3

There Was a Foot Inside the Boot

It's probably worth knowing that the boot contained a foot belonging to the Human Bookseller With A Beard that was attached to a leg belonging to the Human Bookseller With A Beard that was attached to the body belonging to the Human Bookseller With A Beard – basically the Human Bookseller With A Beard was blocking our way in.

'Oh no,' the Human Bookseller With A Beard boomed, shaking his beardy head at us. '*You're* not coming in today.'

He pointed to a square cork noticeboard by the door which said 'Banned By This Bookshop' at the top. There on the board was a picture of a pair of mucky wellington boots caked in a thick layer of mud and dog poop.

And next to it was a photo of me and Dave.

The Human Bookseller With A Beard took a step towards us, forcing us to fall back before we became pigeon pancakes under his ginormous feet, then slammed the door shut.

As a pigeon entering a bookshop, it's important to note that there are two types of bookseller you might meet.

The **Human Bookseller who loves pigeons**: they will let you in, take selfies with you, feed you straight out of their lunchboxes and try and build you a book fort so you can have a nap. If you make a mess, they find you delightful and sweet.

And then there is the **Human Bookseller With A Beard** type: they do not like pigeons. They think you are germ-infested bags of twigs, ruining their customers' experience in their shop and they believe it is their duty to humankind to throw you out.

Unfortunately for us, we had met with the Human Bookseller With A Beard again.

With the door shut tight and no other way in, Dave started to peck at the wooden frame.

'It's no use!' he cried.

He stuck his face up against the glass window, staring longingly at the cash register inside the shop.

'That's where my beloved biscuits are, Skipper,' he wept.

'*Our* biscuits, Dave,' I corrected.

'That's what I said,' he moaned.

I flew up to check for open windows. There were none. I checked for broken roof tiles we might be able to squeeze through, but the entire shop appeared to be pigeon-proof.

'Skipper, we need to get in!' Dave squawked at me.

At least that's what I thought he said. His cries were being drowned out by the sound of a van reversing down the alley by the shop.

It was the postman!

As a pigeon meeting a postie, it's important to note that there are two types of post people.

The **postie who loves pigeons**: they will let you hitch a ride in their van, take selfies with you, feed you straight out of their lunchboxes and try to build you a parcel fort so you can have a nap on the passenger seat. If you make a mess, they find you delightful and sweet.

And then there is the **Postie With A Beard** type: they do not like pigeons. They think you are germ-infested bags of spoons about to poo on their postal van and ruin their day and they believe it is their duty to humankind to get you off the streets.

Unfortunately for us, it was the Postie With A Beard, but fortunately he hadn't spotted us.

'Come on,' I yelled at Dave, pulling him away from the window where he'd left a misty imprint of his face on the glass.

We tracked the sound of the van to the side of

the shop where we watched the Postie unload his parcels

'There's a back door!' I cried, as we spotted the Human Bookseller With A Beard open it wide for the Postie.

As the two of them spoke, distracted by the towering pile of boxes, Dave and I snuck inside, past the Humans.

'That Human Bookseller With A Beard thinks he's so clever,' Dave mocked. 'He can't outwit a pigeon.'

'I don't know,' I said cautiously, hurrying on quickly so we could put some distance between us and the Humans.

'Stop being such a Dovey Downer, Skipper,' Dave sang. He danced across the floor, slowing us down to the pace of a sleepwalking doughnut. 'We'll be feathers-deep in a pile of jammy biscuits soon!'

'We should get moving,' I said, trying to nudge my friend on. 'Those two could be right behind us.'

'Don't worry!' Dave reassured me. 'That Human Bookseller With A Beard hasn't got a clue we're here. We've got plenty of time—'

And then everything went dark.

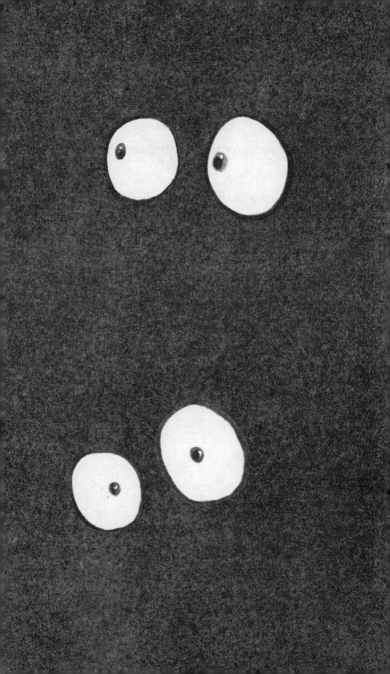

4
The ~~Three~~ Two ~~little~~ Reasonable-Sized Pig̶eons

'I've got you now!' came the muffled squeals of the Human Bookseller With A Beard.

'What's happening?' Dave panicked in the darkness.

'I think we're trapped in a box,' I said, finding it hard to keep the terrified wobble out of my voice.

The box was being shoved across the floor. With every shove, Dave and I leaped forward so we wouldn't be hit on the bottom by a cardboard wall.

'That's it!' Dave bellowed, when the box finally came to a halt. 'I will not let this cardboard box stop me from getting my biscuits.'

He started to boot the box, kicking up his claws, landing hard on his bum each time. He looked like a potato rolling down a flight of stairs.

'It's no use,' he cried, rubbing his sore bottom. 'I've been defeated by the box!'

'Wait,' I calmed my friend, trying hard not to laugh as he looked more and more like a potato. I realised then that light was streaming into the box. 'Look!'

Dave had managed to pierce three tiny holes in the card. I peered through and could see that the Human Bookseller With A Beard was talking on his phone.

'. . . those pigeons will be gone,' the Human Bookseller With A Beard muttered into the phone.

'How dare he?' Dave said, ducking under my wing to peek through the hole beneath. 'I'm not going anywhere.'

Angrier and more clawry, Dave flung himself at the box wall, tearing through the holes and forcing his head out.

'I did it, Skipper,' he cried. 'I escaped.'

Well, his head had escaped at least.

I pecked the opening around his head, pulling it further back until Dave could squeeze through and I could follow. The Human Bookseller With A Beard was still distracted. We took our chance and dashed for the door to the main floor of the bookshop.

Dust floated in shards of light that lit up the tables stacked with books. The smells of oak bookshelves and the sweet musk of yellowing book pages were like finding a warm hot chocolate on a snowy park bench.

'Dave, we could live here amongst the books,' I murmured, running my feathers along the long leather spines of an encyclopaedia collection.

'We'd have to do something about that Human Bookseller With A Beard first,' Dave complained.

Right! I'd forgotten about him. We needed to find a safe place to hide before he came after us again.

We headed for the children's books. It was the best place to camouflage as a pigeon. The bright bunting and colourful covers were the perfect distractions.

My beak fell open as we turned the corner into the magical children's section. I hopped along the rows of adventure books, imagining a couple of pigeons in safari hats travelling across the world in time machines like the heroes in the stories. I skipped down to the funny books, pulling Dave

up to join me as we laughed at the pictures of lionesses in tracksuits and dogs in police hats.

And then there were our favourite books of all – the baking books. Pages upon pages of tasty snacks that made a pigeon's beak water and a Dave peck at a page to see if they tasted of paper or cupcakes. (It was paper.)

Yes. I could absolutely live in a bookshop like this.

Dave and I picked a spot by the fairy tales and

tried our hardest to look like a couple of books. But we hadn't been there long before we heard the Human Bookseller With A Beard huffing and puffing around the corner.

'There you are, you little skyrats,' he exclaimed, spotting us on our little wooden shelf not looking like books at all. 'Get away from my precious books!'

'Oh no,' Dave squawked. 'Not again.'

The Human stalked towards us, never once breaking his gaze with Dave.

'I think it's time to go!' I yelped.

I grabbed Dave and tried to fly up. We didn't get far. I couldn't carry us both. And as we tumbled backwards, arching away from the Human Bookseller's outstretched arms, we tumbled down the back of the bookcase.

With us trapped in the gap between the bookcase and the brick wall and the Human on the other side, he couldn't get at us! His shoulders dropped. He grabbed at us once more but his arm could not reach through the opening.

Dave danced circles in our little brick cave. 'Ha ha! You can't get us,' he teased the bookseller.

The Human sat back. He stared at us. He almost looked like he was about to say something but he didn't. Instead he got up and turned away.

I watched him as he disappeared from sight. As he stepped further away from us, he touched the spine of each book he passed, as though he was a protective Papa Pigeon looking after his baby squabs.

For a moment I felt bad for him. Maybe all he wanted was to protect his books. But then Dave started picking his claws and pinging nail dirt at me so I forgot what I was thinking about.

'We won!' Dave chuckled. He grabbed my shoulder. 'Let's go get our biscuits. That Human won't mess with us again.'

But something told me the Human Bookseller With A Beard was absolutely going to mess with us again.

5

Little Red ~~Riding~~
Flying ~~Hood~~ Hat

As Dave continued flicking out bits of nail jam, I pressed up against the back of the bookcase and listened hard.

There were now at least two Mini Humans in the children's section. They pulled out books three at a time and begged their parents to read them. They laughed at all the silly voices and stopped the story every other word to ask a question. It reminded me of when I read to Dave before each nap time.

Beyond the family, I could hear another Human in the travel section asking for recommendations about books.

I listened out for sounds that felt a bit beardy. When I was absolutely sure I couldn't hear the Human Bookseller With A Beard, I poked my beak out around the corner of the bookcase, careful not to be spotted by the curious Mini Humans.

The Human Bookseller was nowhere to be seen.

Maybe Dave was right. Maybe we *had* won.

I squeezed out from behind the bookcase and then had to pull Dave out after me. We inched along the wall slowly, just in case we needed to make a run for our little cave again. The family of Humans had moved to the till with their books and the children's section was all ours again.

'Look at that plate of biscuits,' Dave groaned.

Across the shop floor, by the cash register, was a blue and white polka-dot plate with ten jammy biscuits on top. They were home-made. I could tell. The biscuits looked buttery and glittered with sugar granules, and bright red strawberry jam spilled out of the sides over a vanilla buttercream.

'We need to get over there,' Dave whispered desperately.

I agreed. Those biscuits weren't going to be there long as the queue at the till grew, and the Bookseller serving the customers offered a biscuit to everyone waiting.

'We need a disguise to get across the shop,' I said to Dave.

'How about this?' Dave said, holding up a stuffed toy.

'That's a pigeon!'

'Really?' Dave said, looking at the toy pigeon. 'It looks nothing like me.'

It looked exactly like him.

I ignored my friend and spotted a nearby bear in a red hat. 'This could work,' I suggested to Dave.

I pecked the hat free from the brown bear's head. It toppled to the floor, rolling in circles before stopping. We clambered in, flipped it over our bodies and started our journey across the shop, keeping an eye out for the Human Bookseller With A Beard.

If anyone thought a red hat walking across a bookshop floor was strange, nobody let on.

We dodged ankles and trampling feet and pram wheels and falling books, and made it all the way across to the cash register and the plate of biscuits in our red hat.

At the bottom of the desk, we tucked in behind a box of bookmarks to figure out how to get up to the plate.

'We can't just climb up,' Dave said. And he was right. For once.

For once? I'm always right, Skipper.

Name me one time you were right.

Yesterday.

When?

When we found that double croissant and it was too heavy to move. You said we should take an end each. You were left and I was right.

The shelves up to the plate were too steep to climb. I was going to have to fly up to get the biscuits.

'Use the red-hat disguise,' Dave suggested. 'Once you're up there, throw down the biscuits.'

Just as I was about to take off, Dave let out a strange sound. Like a strangled caw. His eyes were large and his beak wide open. He was transfixed by the sight in front of him.

There, staring back at us, was a ginormous pigeon. It was colossal. The size of a Human but a *pigeon*.

'What a big beak he has,' Dave said, mesmerised.

The pigeon stalked over to us slowly. There was something very familiar about the way it moved.

'What massive eyeballs he's got,' Dave said in awe, making his way towards the pigeon like an alien to the mothership.

The familiar way this pigeon moved was starting to make my tummy feel funny. Like I was about to do a monster-sized pigeon poop.

'What a strange, non-pigeony smell he has,' Dave gawped, getting closer.

The smell! The smell of fake pigeon and a *beard*! I knew this mammoth pigeon!

'What a whopper-sized beard he has, Dave!' I screeched. 'It's the Human Bookseller With A Beard. It's a trap!'

Just as the Human Bookseller With A Beard whipped off his pigeon mask and grabbed for Dave, I scooped up my friend in the red hat and launched with everything I had back towards our bookcase, leaving our biscuits behind.

6
Hansel and Gretel

> Who in pigeon peanut butter are they? This is my story! This chapter is now called Dave and Skipper.

'We were so close,' Dave cried, weeping for the biscuits.

'We were almost so caught,' I replied, relieved to be back in the safety of our cave behind the bookcase.

'Can you believe he tried to impersonate a pigeon?' Dave scoffed. 'How would he like it if I put on a teeny-tiny Human mask and pretended to be all Humany?'

It was hard to get rid of that horrifying image from my head.

'What is that Human's problem?' Dave continued.

'I guess he doesn't want pigeons in his bookshop,' I sighed.

'What's wrong with pigeons in a bookshop?' Dave asked.

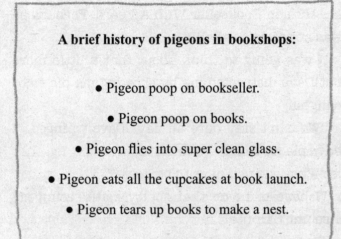

A brief history of pigeons in bookshops:

- Pigeon poop on bookseller.

- Pigeon poop on books.

- Pigeon flies into super clean glass.

- Pigeon eats all the cupcakes at book launch.

- Pigeon tears up books to make a nest.

I could hear the Human Bookseller With A Beard still out on the shop floor. The Mini Humans from earlier were giggling and I couldn't resist sneaking a peek to see what all the fuss was about.

The Human Bookseller With A Beard had flicked the pigeon mask back over his head. I could see now that he was in a bird costume, handing out goodie bags to the little ones.

That feeling I'd had before came back. You know, the one I had right before Dave started flicking nail dirt all over the place. It was back and it was stronger. I wondered if we'd misunderstood the Human Bookseller With A Beard. Perhaps he was not after us at all?

I was going to think about that a little more but Dave distracted me by showing me his right wingpit.

'We can't stay here all day,' Dave whinged. 'I have places to be.'

'Where do you have to be, Dave?'

'I have to be on that spotty plate eating my biscuits, Skipper!'

Dave was right. Not about having places to be, but we *did* have to find a way out without being captured.

'What's that?' Dave said.

His beak was raised high, like he'd caught a whiff of something.

It was the unmistakeable scent of buttery shortbread.

We peeked out from behind the bookcase.

There on the bright yellow table in the children's section was a pile of biscuits. They'd been arranged into a small fort, almost like a house built of biscuits and jam.

'It's my dream home,' Dave gasped.

'It's a trick,' I said, holding my friend back as he tried to push past.

'Why?' Dave squawked. 'Why does everything need to be a trick, Skipper?'

'Because it always is!'

Great globs of saliva dripped from Dave's beak. 'This one is not a trick. I just know it.'

'How many times does a biscuit house just turn up out of nowhere?' I said suspiciously.

'Maybe four or five times?' Dave guessed.

'Never!' I cried. 'It never happens.'

'Fine,' Dave said. 'Maybe it's a trick. Who cares? Let's just go have a little nibble of the roof and then get out of here.'

My tummy churned like an ice-cream maker full of pencil sharpeners. I needed a moment to think.

But it was too late.

'Dave! Wait!'

Dave had never moved so fast. His eyes were fixed on the delicious roof, dusted in powdered sugar.

'Dave! Stop!' I yelled.

He raced to the table, clambering up on a stack of books to reach the stool by the biscuits. He slipped on the shiny surface of the table as he scrambled towards the house.

Before I could warn him, a heavy fairy-tale book slammed down next to Dave, making him

tumble back on to his bottom and knock his head.
'I have you now!' the Human Bookseller With A
Beard cried, clutching a dazed Dave in his hands.

7

Every Good Fairy Tale Needs a ... Panda?

'Skipper!' Dave screeched, as he rubbed his knocked head.

'Don't worry, Dave,' I squawked back. But I couldn't help the feeling of panic bubbling up from my guts. 'I'll go get help!'

A small crowd of shoppers had started to gather around the Human Bookseller With A Beard and my friend. With the Human in a pigeon costume, for a moment it almost looked like a proud pigeon father holding his very tiny baby.

'I knew I should've worn a teeny-tiny Human mask,' Dave squawked. 'He never would've seen me coming.'

I didn't have the heart to tell my friend that everyone would've seen him coming if he had a Human head and a pigeon bottom.

Dave squirmed and flapped as he tried to escape the Human's hands. But it was no use. Years of stacking bookshelves meant the Human Bookseller With A Beard had hands the size of pizzas and a grip as strong as superglue.

With his hands full of Dave, and all the other Humans distracted, I knew I had to take my chance to get out and find help.

I hurled myself into the air, squeezed my eyes shut and dived for the front of the shop. I heard wrapping paper flap beneath me as I soared past the till and straight for the open front door.

I didn't stop until I could feel the cool air in my wings and the delicious scent of books had disappeared. In fact, it had altogether been replaced with the stink of hay and raccoon droppings.

I opened my eyes and nearly fell out of the

sky when I realised I was hovering over the zoo across the road.

In fact, I was hovering right above an enclosure labelled 'LIN AND FU'.

There in the grassy paddocks beyond the gate were two pandas. They were sitting amongst a pile of bamboo, playing what seemed to be a game of 'who can spit the balled-up bit of bamboo the furthest'.

Carefully dodging the oncoming spitballs, I flew down to perch on a branch of the willow tree shading the bears.

'Hello?' I cawed.

'Hello, little pigeon!' the male panda replied.

He turned to his paddock mate. 'Lin, look, it's a pigeon.'

Lin regarded me. 'You're in our game,' she said, waving her paw at the pile of bamboo leaves on the ground. She stood to shoo me away. She was

at least fifteen hundred thousand pigeons tall.

I swallowed hard and stuck my chin out as she wafted her paws at me to move on. I thought of Dave trapped with the Human Bookseller With A Beard. What if he was about to be blitzed into pigeon soup?

'I need your help,' I said to the panda.

Lin eyed me curiously and nodded me on to continue.

'My friend is trapped in the bookshop across the street,' I explained. 'I need someone to help me break him out. He can't fly. He's injured.'

'Someone trapped your friend?' Lin asked. 'A defenceless little injured bird?'

I didn't correct Lin and explain that it was sort of our own fault Dave was trapped because we were at the bookshop to nick biscuits, or that my friend Dave wasn't really that little or defenceless (I'd seen him peck his way into a plastic cabinet of sandwiches at the supermarket). Right now, I needed this ginormous panda to help me out, so I nodded my saddest pigeon nod.

Lin's eyes flashed with anger. I'd seen pandas in books and stories and they always reminded me of massive, happy teddy bears. They were the good in the animal kingdom as opposed to cats, which were the evil.

But this panda was different. Her face was screwed up in fury which somehow made her look more furry, but it was the balled-up fists that let me know she could be a bad panda when she was angry. Little did I know that Lin had history when it came to freeing animals once the bad panda inside her was unleashed.

'Let's go rescue your friend,' she growled, charging towards the zoo gates.

8
Bad Panda to the Rescue!

Lin scooped me up in her furry paws and rolled us both across the road towards the bookshop.

'Do you think we need a plan to get in?' I asked.

'Yes,' she roared. 'Let's go through the front door.'

So we did.

The entire store had emptied apart from a group of schoolchildren gathered in the children's section. The Human Bookseller With A Beard was reading them a book about grizzly bears. The children were so engrossed they didn't notice the massive panda that had just walked through the front door and knocked over the bookmark display.

'Where's your friend?' Lin asked, looking around.

There, next to the Human Bookseller With A Beard, was a small birdcage on a little table. Dave was trapped inside, cowering in the corner.

I pointed Lin towards the children's books. She snuck behind the bookshelves of biographies, holding me close to her chest. We took the next bookcase on the left packed full of travel guides and followed the book racks round to the leather-clad novels by the children's section.

As we got closer, I could see Dave.

I blinked hard and rubbed my eyes with my wings.

There he was.

I blinked again.

Dave was tucked away in the corner of the cage.

Only he wasn't actually cowering at all.

Instead, he was curled up on a blanket, listening to the story. There were crumbs at the bottom of the cage. And Dave was clinging on to a jammy bit of shortbread like it was a teddy bear.

What's more, Dave was giggling along to the story!

We'd been wrong!

The Human Bookseller With A Beard didn't hate us.

He had just given Dave food and shelter.

He'd only wanted to clear the area for the children's story time.

And I was just about to let a bad panda loose in his bookshop!

'STOP!' I screeched at Lin.

It was too late.

The huge bear charged at the cage, knocking it over and freeing Dave, who quickly jumped into the arms of the stunned Human Bookseller With A Beard. Children cheered as teachers screamed and panicked, snatching kids to safety away from the angry bear.

'It's time you were in a cage of your own,' Lin growled at the Human Bookseller With A Beard.

He didn't understand a word of panda and hugged Dave close to his body, protecting my friend from what seemed like an out-of-control, ravenous bear.

I swooped in and caught the top of Dave's head.

'Come on!' I screeched.

We half flew and half hopped across the heads of the schoolchildren as Lin shoved bookcases together to create a bookcase prison for the Human Bookseller With A Beard.

'What is going on?' Dave squawked.

'We're here to save you,' I said, scrambling to safety as books rained down from the shelves. 'I went to get help.'

'So you found a panda?!' Dave shrieked.

'I needed to rescue you!'

'I was fine!' Dave yelled over the noise of frantic teachers. 'It turns out the Human Bookseller With A Beard is all right. He gave me that entire plate of biscuits and let me pick out my own birdcage. I had a bed and a floor to eat off!'

We watched in horror as the bookshop was ravaged by the panda, and a bunch of hysterical teachers and a class of wild schoolchildren ran riot. Pages were ripped clean from books as children went berserk with paper-plane missiles, and three teachers huddled on the floor sobbing for their parents to pick them up.

'Whoops,' I said to Dave.

9

And They Lived Happily Ever After. Probably. Mostly. Maybe. The Human Bookseller With A Beard Might've Needed a Day Off Work to Recover

Once we'd told Lin about the misunderstanding, she stopped her mad rampage and pulled the terrified Human Bookseller With A Beard up out of his bookcase cage.

'Sorry about that,' she said, dusting him off.

She waved us all goodbye and headed out of the bookshop back towards the zoo.

Children were being taken away by very loud parents who were shouting and crying, even though their children looked like they'd just had the best day of their lives. Staff rushed around trying to put the bookshop back to its original state and the Human Bookseller With A Beard was still trembling as someone tried to hand him a cup of tea.

'We should probably go,' I whispered to Dave, nudging him towards the door.

'Do you think the Human Bookseller With A Beard is going to eat those biscuits?' Dave mused, as we watched the Human take a very shaky sip of tea from the cup clattering on the saucer in his jittery hands.

'Dave!'

'What?' Dave said. 'It'd be a shame if they go to waste.'

'I think we've probably proved why pigeons shouldn't be allowed into bookshops. Let's not make it worse by taking his last two biscuits.'

'I think the only thing we proved was why *pandas* shouldn't be allowed into bookshops,' Dave replied.

'Dave!'

'Fine,' my friend grumbled. 'Let's go home.'

We headed out of the bookshop, across the large green doormat and towards the bus stop.

DIARIES

2023

Please Pay Here

BOOK
LoVer

WORLD
BOOK
DAY

BOOK

Dave suddenly stopped and put a wing up on my shoulder. His eyes were wide.

'What's wrong?' I asked.

'Skipper,' he whispered. 'Look!'

He pointed ahead of us. A huge silver and gold balloon arch was being installed at a shop a few doors down. Ribbon had been tied across the front window and a small flock of Humans had gathered outside.

'No, Skipper,' Dave said, tapping my head. 'Look up!'

I tilted my head to the sky and saw the sign hanging above the new shop. The gold letters spelled out a familiar word. This was going to be a new *bookshop*.

SHOP

'I think we should make one final stop before we head home, Skipper,' Dave said, grinning at me.

Oh pigeon fluff, here we go again ...

I have a great joke about pandas.
Yeah?
Why did the panda wear slippers?
Pandas don't wear slippers.
You're meant to say, 'Why did the panda wear slippers?'
But you just said that.
I know. That's how jokes work.

Enjoy a sneaky pigeon peek
at the first chapter of . . .

1
The Beginning . . .

Dave and me were on a routine croissant heist. It was something we'd done at least a hundred times before.

In fact, the first time I met Dave was on a croissant heist. Back then, Dave told me he had just won a Medal of the Brave which he wore all the time. (Though I

heard a rumour later it was just a bottle top that had got stuck to him with a piece of chewing gum when he got caught in a bin bag once).

Dave was swooping in from the opposite side of the pond when we both spotted a half-eaten croissant abandoned under a bench. We dived down, crashing towards the same gap between two planks of bench wood, and landed at the exact same time.

There we were, dangling upside down, stuck in the bench, when a huge goose grabbed our croissant and waddled off with it. A goose, for Bird's sake.

We never did get that croissant back, did we?
Dave!
What?
Do you want me to tell this story?
Sorry, Skipper. On you go.

What I was about to say was – we never got our croissant back. We caught up to the goose just fine, but let me tell you something about geese. They are far bigger up close than when you see them in the distance. And they are very pecky. We were grateful to leave that fight with all our feathers.

Dave and I have been friends ever since.

Where was I? Ah, yes. The day we met Mean Cat. Our one hundredth croissant heist.

It was a bright, sunny morning, and me and Dave were starving. Peck-your-own-feathers-off starving. All we'd had for breakfast were the wet breadcrumbs a Little Human had already chewed and spat out, and a teeny-tiny piece of an iced bun we'd managed to steal from a duck.

That's when I spotted a Human Lady. We couldn't believe our luck. Everyone knows that Human Ladies like to carry around crusts with them. Dave said that's what their handbags were for.

Dave and I pattered over trying to look friendly and hungry . . .

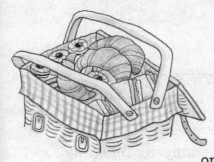

As predicted, the Human Lady popped the clasp on her picnic basket. There was more than just bread! Inside we spied a feast of croissants, sandwiches and biscuits. And they were the biscuits with the jam in the middle. My favourites.

'Follow me,' I said, shuffling closer.

The Human Lady spotted us. 'Good morning.'

We didn't say anything back because we couldn't speak Human.

'Would you like some croissant?' she said.

Of course we would.

She read our minds and tore off a piece

of golden-brown flaky pastry, throwing it towards us.

The sweet crumbs tumbled to our feet and we gobbled up as much as we could, filling our aching bellies. We inched closer to the basket, hoping to pinch a pastry or two for supper later.

'You two must be hungry,' the Human Lady said, throwing us broken bits of bread.

Dave cooed and hopped even closer to the basket. 'Come on,' he said, nodding at me.

I caught a whiff of something awful. 'What's that?'

'What?'

'That smell . . .'

'Sorry,' said Dave, fanning his bottom. 'I think it's that biryani from the bin I had last night.'

'Not *that* smell—'

The stink got stronger and stronger, burning my nostrils and stinging my eyes.

'Stop!' the Human Lady shouted. *'Stop!'*

A flash of ginger and white shot out from behind the basket . . .